Going Raw, The Collection

Danii Dezire

Published by Danii Dezire, 2015.

This is a work of fiction. Similarities to real people, places, or events are entirely coincidental.

GOING RAW, THE COLLECTION

First edition. September 7, 2015.

ISBN: 979-8201358754

Written by Danii Dezire.

Going Raw, The Collection

by

Danii Dezire

If any of the sexual situations within this story have occurred in your life consider yourself lucky.

Red & Raw (Going Raw)

"I've had it with cheating men!" cried Sadie into her cell phone.

Her friend, Emma, who was on the receiving end of this declaration, tried to calm her down. "Oh, Sadie, honey," she said. "They're not all bad. Some of them are genuinely cowed enough to know they shouldn't mess around with curvy goddesses like us."

Neither woman felt such a statement was close to the truth, but it certainly helped Sadie a little to think it was. At least for the moment. Was she ready to give up on men all together? No. There was one special kind she had never experienced before. Tall, dark, and... well more dark. All over. But would it ever happen before she took a vow of celibacy and joined a convent?

Sadie paced her apartment living room. "I don't care to find out anymore. So many games, so many lies. A woman can't get anything honest from someone who owns a penis. They just can't be trusted."

She had reason to be angry. Andre, her boyfriend... ex-boyfriend... had just admitted to her, not fifteen minutes ago, that he had been unfaithful to her for the last two months of their relationship. With some waitress at a bar he frequented.

The coward had told her over the phone, too. He didn't have the nerve, or the balls, to tell her to her face. She would have liked to have punched him! Or at least scratched his eyes out. Yet, the snake had the nerve to say she needed to lose a little bit of weight! Sadie considered her voluptuous curves one of her greatest assets. The opinionated bastard.

Emma continued to try and calm her friend down. "Yeah, they're scum. They can't be trusted. Maybe you should just, I dunno, maybe take a break from serious relationships for a little bit. I know this just happened and all, but maybe this was for the best."

Sadie had paced into the bedroom and caught her reflection in the closet mirror. She was still in a bathrobe, having showered in preparation for going out with Carl that evening. She gave her body an appraising once over. She was hot dammit! Nice curves, large and pendulous breasts, with a stellar smile. Why would any man in his right mind even entertain the idea of screwing around behind her back? Especially *this* lovely back! She turned and lifted up the robe exposing a pleasantly shaped ass. Nice and roomy, she thought to herself.

No more of this honey-dew for him!

"I know, I know," Sadie said. "It just hurts. I thought we had something truly meaningful. But I guess it wasn't meaningful enough." She gave her own ass a smack and was pleased with the way it shook. "Maybe I should just pick up some random piece of meat at the bar and screw the hell out of it." Preferably a *big and black* piece of meat. God, did she need to get fucked by a big dick for once. Andre, although admittedly skilled, certainly lacked in the size department.

She needed to trade up, dammit!

"Yes!" Emma shouted. "Nothing better than cheap meaningless sex with a stranger to help you get through times of trouble. Maybe you should get yourself a good healthy dose of dark chocolate, if you know what I mean."

"Chocolate is good for your health, you know?" Sadie said.

"Nine out of ten sex therapists recommend a good dose of chocolate daily. Helps with the skin."

Both women laughed.

Sadie said, "Jesus, do I need to get laid."

"I ain't arguing with that."

Just then the downstairs buzzer rang.

"Who's that?" asked Emma.

"Oh, shoot. I was expecting a package delivered today for work." Andre had called her right after she got the a call-confirmation, asking if she would be home. She buzzed in whoever it was without answering.

"Wait a second, sister," said Emma, conspiratorially. "What if he's a hunk?"

Sadie scoffed. "No, it's always this little fat guy who smells of sweat and cheese."

"You should *do* him!"

"No way!" Sadie shuddered. Just the thought of it made her skin crawl.

"Or, it could be someone different. A moonlighting underwear model."

Sadie's brow furrowed. "Wow, you have quite the imagination. Well, if that were the case, he'd get one hell of a tip outta me, tonight."

"That a girl!" cried Emma.

Sadie was only half joking. It would take a lot to get her to indulge in a casual quickie with a stranger.

There was a knock at the door. Sadie took a moment to look herself over in the living room mirror. The robe hung half open, so she cinched it closed. It accentuated her voluptuous breasts. Her legs were bare for all to see. The robe only just covered her magnificient ass. She hadn't put on any underwear after she finished showering, and there certainly wasn't any time now to put some on.

I do look damn sexy, though, she thought to herself. At least mister chubby from the pizza place will get a little bit of an eye full.

While she walked to the door, Emma was chanting in the phone, "Hot sex! Hot sex! Hot sex!"

Sadie could only roll her eyes. As if.

She peered through the peek hole.

A tall dashing hunk of a man was standing out there. Holding a boxed package. Her boxed package. And even better, he was dark. Dark all over.

"Uh," was all Sadie was able to say.

Emma immediately pounced. "What? WHAT?!"

Sadie found herself whispering, her eye glued to the hole, drinking in the beefcake outside. "It's not the usual guy. He's..." *Gorgeous*.

"So? Is he handsome, or just handsome enough?" asked Emma, intrigued with her friend's change of tone. "Either will do for now."

"Wait," Sadie said, realization dawning on her. "I recognize him. He's friend of Andre's! We've never met before." But she certainly noticed him. It was at some sort of fund raising event. He had been standing with some other handsome black men.

"Honey," said Emma, excited. "This could be the perfect chance for revenge sex! Do your ex-boyfriend's buddy!"

Sadie realized she had been staring at him entirely too long. She took a deep breath and opened the door.

The peephole view did not do this walking Greek God justice. Tall, chiseled features, and perfectly muscled, he gave Sadie a pearly white smile.

"Hi," he said. "I have a package delivery for a Sadie?"

Sadie was momentarily speechless. She was also alarmed to feel a dampness grow between her upper thighs.

"Yeah," she managed to stammer smiling, still a little shocked. She stepped back, letting him inside. She closed the door behind him.

She had forgotten her cell phone was in her free hand, until she dimly heard Emma cry out: "Do him! Screw his brains out! Give him a tip he'll never forget! Revenge sex!"

Sadie quickly hung up. The courier man... stud, crooked a questioning eyebrow. She managed not to blush. "My friend is being annoying," she finally said, and immediately felt ridiculous.

He continued smiling politely, "Our delivery service has that effect on folks." She noticed his beautiful brown eyes glanced down at her robe, and then at her legs before quickly returning to her eyes again.

She was surprised to find herself thrilled at this.

"You're not the usual courier guy." *Thank the Lord!*

"Oh, you probably get Peter," his voice was deep, confident. The kind you wouldn't mind having whispering instructions in your ear. "He called in sick so I had to pick up the slack."

She nodded, dully. This guy was a lot to take in. She suddenly found herself wondering just how much that would be, and in how many positions. "I've never seen you before. Are you new there?"

"New? Oh, more than that. I'm the owner."

She looked down at the company name on the package. It said Tony's Package Delivery Service. "You're Tony?" she said, incredulous.

"The big boss man himself," he said with a confident grin.

She found she was most definitely horny, now. Maybe there was a package he could delivery for her, and not the one in his hands.

"Do you know Andre?" she asked impulsively.

Tony thought for a moment, and his eyes brightened. "Yes, I do. Been an acquaintance for years. Why?" Then his eyes widened. "Ah, I know you. You're Andre's girlfriend."

Sadie arched a brow at him. "Ex-girlfriend," she said, putting on hand on an ample hip.

Now Tony looked genuinely intrigued. "Really?" He gave her body the once over, and this absolutely thrilled Sadie. "His loss." He said shaking his head. The statement sounded genuinely honest.

Sadie smiled and said, "And maybe someone else's gain?" She was struck with a strong impulse and felt an overwhelming urge to act on it. Emma was right. Meaningless sex with a stranger could be exactly what she needs right now. Especially with this particular handsome black stranger.

Fuck it, she thought to herself, *I'm a single vivacious woman. And I want a man. THIS man!*

“Oh, please bring it in the living room,” she said, walking away from him. He more or less had to follow. As she turned she sneaked a look at his wedding finger. Barren.

Good.

She also noted his eyes fell on her butt as she talked to him over her shoulder. *Gotcha!*

“Right over there, please,” she pointed at the big coffee table which was between the couch and the easy chair. There was a plate of warmed up pizza she was nibbling on, sitting on the table.

Tony gave a short nod to her as he passed. She inhaled his wake as he did so, and liked the hint of his cologne, and the slight tinge of sweat. Most likely from working hard most of the night.

She yearned to make him sweat some more.

Tony placed the package on the table, and as he turned toward her, Sadie quickly undid her robes, and let them fall to the floor. She put her hands on her curvy hips and bent a knee slighting for enticing emphasis.

He froze, eyes locked on her naked form. She was sexy as all hell, and she could see he thought the same.

“Well, Tony of Tony's Delivery Service,” she said, with fire in her eyes, and a seductive tone in her voice. “I have a way I can pay you properly for that package.”

His jaw dropped, and his eyes roved over her. He was appropriately shell shocked, and took several moments to compose himself.

Who could blame him?

“I, uh...” he stammered.

Deciding to take her initiative even further she didn't want him to have to decide on his own. She walked forward, breasts jiggling hypnotically, and grabbed at his t-shirt. He only flinched just slightly, as if his brain was only now catching up with unfolding events, but he smiled and yielded.

He chuckled and raised his arms so she could pull the it off of him.

His chest did not disappoint. Beautiful dark skin everywhere. Ridged muscles lined his body and stomach. His pectorals were the size of dinner plates and his arms were hard as tempered steel, and almost as thick as her own thighs.

Sadie ran her hands over his barrelled chest. "You lift a lot of heavy packages to get a body like that?" she asked teasingly.

"Something like that," he said. His hands rubbed her shoulders, and up and down her arms. Then he cupped her ample breasts, squeezing them. She found his hands were calloused and strong, just the way she liked them.

She grabbed at his belt and undid it with a playful grunt. He smiled and let her work at it. When unbuckled, she unzipped his fly, then squatted down in front of him, pulling his pants down. She managed to work them to his hips, and with one final tug, yanked them down to his knees.

It was then that a huge black dick popped out of them, partially engorged. The sudden motion of the pants had freed this large piece of meat from its lair, and it swung out and hit her in the side of the nose.

"Oh, my God!" She gasped. He smiled down at her. She blinked in astonishment. "I don't remember ordering this!" She giggled, amazed.

"It's an extra service. For hot, sexy customers only," he said.

She pulled off his shoes, and then aided him in removing his pants from his ankles. She then turned her attention to the now large erect penis in front of her, demanding attention.

Grabbing it eagerly, she stroking it up and down, marvelling at its thickness, and heft. Stealing her courage, she then put it in her mouth, and started to suck. It was large. She had dreamt of managing a cock of this size before. Now she could.

Tony sighed with the sudden feel of her warm wet mouth on his prick, and the feel of her lips moving up and down his shaft. Because of his size, the sound of her slurping and occasional gagging was more prominent.

Up and down she worked him. Long minutes of concentrated effort, with her mouth made his dick glisten with her spit, creating a slight foam at its base. Some spit eventually dribbled down to his balls to dangle there in an elastic string.

Satisfied she had properly welcomed him into her home, she leaned back a bit for a breather, and gasped.

She motioned to the easy chair, "Sit down. I have an idea."

"I like your ideas so far," he said with wide appreciative eyes. He did as he was told.

She turned to the still-hot pizza slice on the table and stuck her fingers in it. As she tried to pick at a ring of green pepper she squealed girlishly from its heat. Finding one that suited her needs, she turned towards him, and his eyes widened at what she had in mind.

Gingerly, she broke it at one point, then wrapped the green pepper around the base of his thick cock. Because he was so well shaved, it rested against his dark skin and he hissed slightly, but not with great pain.

"You okay?" she asked coyly.

"Oh, yeah," he said through gritted teeth. "I knew my customers were hot but not *this* hot."

She grinned up at him, then swirled her tongue around his prick. She took his dick in her mouth, and slowly worked her way down his length, occasionally pausing to wiggle her head back and forth to help it past the hook at the back of her throat. He gasped, as her tongue poked out of the bottom of her gaping mouth. His girth had forced her mouth wide, stretching her lips around him. Spittle gathered in sticky strands at the corners.

With amazing patience, she neither gagged, or pulled back. She gazed up at him with big eyes, and her tongue prodded the green pepper until she managed to catch it. Then, very slowly, she slid back up his length, green pepper in tow.

Sucking him at the tip, the green pepper dangled from her mouth. Then she leaned back, plucking it in her fingers and smiling at him triumphantly.

"Impressive!" He said, laughing. "My turn to do a trick."

He eased her up off her knees, and had her sit in the easy chair, this time. She spread her legs by hooking her knees over the arms, exposing her very well shaved, and *very* wet pussy to him. She rubbed at her clit playfully.

"Do as you please, delivery boy," she said while teething the tip of one of her fingers.

"Oh, I will," Tony returned. With one finger he dipped into the tomato sauce of the pizza slice. Careful to get enough, he then slowly spread it around her pussy, smearing it completely with sauce.

It was her turn to grit her teeth from the heat, as he worked his fingers around her clit. Then he leaned forward, and with strong hands firmly holding her legs wide at the thighs, he started to lick.

Up and down, then all around, he licked and slurped. When a little sauce dripped down into the slight hollow at her asshole, he slurped it up. He then stayed there, rimming her asshole with his tongue.

Sadie gasped with pleasure, squeezing her big tits, pinching at their erect nipples.

Then he returned his attention to her pussy, taking long deliberate licks, making sure he wasn't finished until it was completely cleaned of tomato sauce.

Tony grinned up at her and said, "Now that special sauce tasted damn good."

She smiled back and said, "Glad to be on your menu."

He then stood, cock still hard and ready. He leaned forward, so he was hovering over her, and bent his massive dick downwards as far as it would go. He stuck his fat prick into her waiting pussy. She gasped, and grabbed onto his hips. He paused, and said, "Can I make an express delivery, ma'am?"

"Please do!" Sadie said.

And with that, he suddenly slammed the entire length of his long dick deep inside her. She gasped with the hard penetration. He then lifted his ass up again, so his entire length was nearly unsheathed from her, and slammed it down again.

Over and over he did this, getting faster and faster. She moaned with each pelvic thrust. Long wonderful minutes passed as he slammed her pussy again and again. She felt all her flesh jiggle and shake with each pounding motion. Eventually, the intensity got to be so much Sadie's eyes rolled upwards showing only their whites.

Tony reached around her neck and pulled against her head slightly, so as to cut off some of the circulation. She gasped for air while he continued his relentless hammering. He eased off her head only when she seemed close to passing out.

Then he slowed, making easy gyrating motions with his hips. Tony wanted to give her a little time to recover before giving her what was about to happen next.

When she seemed okay, he slipped out of her and her pussy gave a wet fart. He then turned her around and pushed her on the chair so her upper body leaning against the back of it. Her beautiful tits hung down over the back edge. Tony perched behind her, and smacked her incredible ass. It shook pleasantly.

Then he eased his dick into her pussy again, which was now sopping wet. Making sure Sadie was firmly pressed up against the chair, hands holding her wide hips tightly, he began to pump back and forth. Each time he slammed her ass she grunted with the force of it. He could feel the bottom of his cock rub hard against the inside of her and he knew she felt it, too.

Again, he was relentless in his pounding. Over and over. She gasped and moaned and dug her fingers into the chair. She was almost certain he was going to pound her straight through it.

The apartment filled with the ceaseless smacking of flesh on flesh. Punctuated with their moans of pleasure.

Eventually, he grabbed her arms, and pulled them back by the elbows, forcing her to arch her back. Her long blond hair dangled down to almost brush against the small of her back, and shook with each hard thrust. He began to slam against her even harder and she moaned more deeply.

On the other side of the living room was a mirror. In the reflection, he could see her huge tits moving with the harsh pounding rhythm. Her mouth was open, eyes were closed, and her brow was furrowed with gritting pleasure.

Over and over; again and again Tony tapped that ass, until he could see that she was getting red where their flesh smacked against one an other.

He could not keep up this relentless pace. With both the feeling of him rubbing wetly inside her, and seeing her wonderfully firm flesh vibrating with his effort, he found himself about to explode.

"I'm gonna cum!" he practically shouted.

Quickly, Sadie pulled her body forward so as to unsheathe his dick from her, and she spun around. He stood, stroking his cock vigorously. She placed the bottom of her open mouth against the base of his swollen prick. Her tongue tickled at it eagerly, and her eyes stared up at him with hunger.

He stroked faster, and soon exploded with a loud moan. He semen spat out all over her; many hot squirts into her mouth which slid down her tongue and pooled at the back of her throat. Over her face in long sticky strands that splayed across her cheeks and forehead. In the corner of one eye, down her chin, and he even got some in her blond hair.

As he sagged with completion, she made a dramatic show of swallowing.

She smacked her mouth, and rolled her tongue around her lips, getting every white bit. A long thick strand still hung from her chin as she grinned widely at him.

"Mmmm," she said. "I love me some brown sugar." *God damn, revenge sex tasted so good!*

She then grabbed his dick again, and sucked it as his erection faded, nursing the last of his load. She wanted every little bit of that special sauce.

It was while she was doing this, and looking up at the exhausted pleasure in his face, that she made a wondrous conclusion:

She needed to get courier service more often, dammit!

END

Rough & Raw (Going Raw)

"Committing crime gets me seriously wet," Sophia said. "So what are you gonna do about it?"

Shotgun in one hand, a box of bullets in the other, Marcus paused. He looked at Sophia who had just came out of the shower. She was wrapped in a towel which did nothing to cover her voluptuous, sexy form. She flopped onto the squeaky hotel bed, dark wet hair sticking to her bare shoulders.

"Can't, babe," he said. "No time. You know that don't you?" He sat on the corner of the bed and started to load rounds into the shotgun. Each one done with a methodical sense of purpose.

Sophia managed a pout, sliding one hand up under the back of his shirt. His dark flesh was wonderfully warm to the touch; hard and muscular, like he was cut from black marble. "We have a little extra time. The manager always arrives at the same exact time. We've seen him."

Marcus tried to focus on his task but found it difficult as her caress stoked his inner flame. Hitting this particular bank had been Sophia's idea. He could tell she was excited about it and needed to let some of that out. He pretended to consider her request. "I dunno," he said.

She smiled. He caved to her desires so easily. She watched for a few moments as he loaded the weapon. Marcus had been her sister's boyfriend for several years, but his criminal activities eventually put a serious strain on their relationship. Sophia actually found it a turn on. Now Marcus was all hers.

His muscular forearms seriously turned her on. Even with his dark skin tone she could easily make out the sleeved tattoos which extended right down to the wrists. Images of coiled serpents, pillars of colourful fire and leering demonic skulls. She could gaze at them all day.

Better yet, Sophia preferred if they were wrapped around her all day. Holding her close. "You like that gun more than me?" she teased.

"Never," he said. "But to keep us flush with cash we need to focus on the job." He offered her a commiserating smile. "After we're finished, babe. I promise."

Marcus loaded the last shell and stood, pulling away from her. It made her unhappy. "I'll give you something to point that at," Sophia said.

With that she pushed herself to a kneeling on the bed, and slowly removed the towel. With a flourish, she cast the towel away.

His eyes took her in. Her incredible curvy form, still glowing slightly from the shower, beckoned to him even more so than any bank vault could.

A detailed tattoo of a black panther was on one shoulder; it's feline form extended down the supple slope of her ample breast, its jaws opened, as if ready to bite the perky pink nipple.

Smiling, she put her hands on her hips, the motion causing her large tits to jiggle pleasantly. "Care for some pre-robbery fun?"

Damn! He thought. *What a fine piece of ass!*

Marcus jammed the last round into the shotgun. "Hell, yeah. Why not? We can make time."

He was about to put the shotgun down onto the nightstand when Sophia motioned for him not to.

"No, I wanna do something," she said.

"What?"

"Something different." Sophia laid on her back, her knees pointed towards Marcus. With a wicked grin she open her legs, the angle of her thighs made is crotch ache.

Exposed to him in all its beautiful, wet glory was her pussy.

Curious, he asked, "What did you have in mind, girl?"

She grinned. "Got a holster for that gun of yours, mister."

Marcus was perplexed. "Shotguns don't need holsters." He held it up giving it a comical look of confusion.

Sophia giggled. "That one does." Her hands moved down her belly, past the small triangle thatch of pubic hair, and down to her pussy. She spread her pussy lips with her fingers, exposing the wet pink within. "Right here," she said.

Marcus laughed. "Think it's to big." He arched an eyebrow at her. "Won't fit."

"Then that's your problem," she said. She started to gently play with her clit as she looked up at him with hooded eyes. "You have experience jamming big things into tight, wet spaces."

Marcus' eyes went wide. "God. You are a wild one, aren't you, babe?" He put one knee up on the mattress so he was between her open legs, her feet hooking around his waist.

"You know it," she said.

He eased the shotgun forward finding himself getting aroused with the image of the shotgun between beautiful naked legs, and inches away from her hot pussy.

Sophia grabbed at the shotgun with both hands. For a moment Marcus thought she was going to thrust it inside her.

Instead, she started to slowly run her hands up and down the barrel. She jerked the shotgun like this for long moments, pretending it was his cock.

Gradually she jerked at it faster and faster. One hand cupped and explored the barrel opening, her fingers probing inside.

She gave him a half smile. "Don't blow your load just yet." She placed one foot on his wide shoulder. Toyed his ear with her toes.

Marcus was positively salivating at that point. He wanted to cast the shotgun aside and fuck her right then and there.

As if sensing his intentions, Sophia stopped masturbating the long barrel and slowly drew it closer to her.

As if hypnotized Marcus could only watch.

She gently ran the edge of the barrel up the length of her pussy. The soft wet lips parted slightly to this intrusion. When she reached her clit, she circled the barrel around it. First clockwise for several slow strokes, then the other way. Her head pushed back against the mattress, big succulent tits quivering. Her nipples her hard and incredibly erect.

Then she slowly ran the barrel edge down her pussy, this time pressing against her flesh a little harder. Again, her lips parted, but exposed more.

Marcus could see pussy juice sticking to the barrel. He wanted very much to suck it all up, but resisted. He concentrated on holding the gun steady and enjoyed the show.

There barrel seemed to catch at the wider bottom edge of her wet cunt, but Sophia continued downward. She angled her legs back until her ankles were up near her own ears. Her little brown asshole presented itself to Marcus. It puckered slightly, as if winking at him.

Flexible girl, Marcus thought.

She then firmly pressed the double barrels against her bare taint. When she removed it he could see the indelible impression of the double barrel openings in her skin, like a figure eight.

Further down she moved it.

Marcus started to sweat. The shotgun quivered a little in his grasp.

"Don't lose your cool now, big boy," Sophia breathed.

Marcus strengthened his resolve. The gun stopped shaking.

Past the taint, Sophia eased the barrel edge over her asshole. Its exploration continuing over this lustful landscape.

She circled her asshole with it, over and over. Occasionally, she would flex her anus, open and closed, with ever complete circle. Her breathing was getting heavier.

Unable to help himself, Marcus guided the barrel until it was directly on the opening.

Sophia smiled. "Spit!" she commanded.

Happy to oblige, Marcus leaned forward over the gun barrel until his nose touched the bottom fleshy part of her pussy. With his mouth, he slowly let out a long gob of saliva. It landed on the gun barrel and slide down over Sophia's asshole. Unsatisfied, he spit some more. He used the barrel to spread the spit around her anus until it gleamed in the hotel room's ruddy lighting.

"Now stick it in," Sophia whispered.

Slowly, with almost glacial like movements, Marcus helped her push the barrel edge into her ass. At first it seemed to resist the foreign object outright, but Marcus knew Sophia loved anal sex, and he had loosened her up that way on many occasions.

With some gentle prodding the edge of the barrel slipped in. Her anus clasped its smooth metal almost hungrily.

Marcus chuckled. "Fuck yeah!" This was impressive. Sophia always could get her freak on.

With the help of his spit, the barrel slide into her. Just a few centimetres. Then he pulled it back, but not enough to pop out. Then back in again. The firm grasp of her asshole clung to the barrel almost possessively.

Several times they did this. Then, almost without warning, Sophia pushed the barrel further inside her, several inches. She paused. Marcus was beside himself with amazement. Her was this voluptuous little sex goddess, naked in front of him, with a gun stuffed in her bung hole.

"I am one lucky fucker," he said aloud.

Sophia didn't respond. Her concentration was on getting the barrel further into her pliable flesh. In and out she moved it. Long lengths it slid. Her asshole now fully accepting the barrel's form; enveloping it completely with its movements.

Lost in concentration, Marcus didn't hear Sophia speak to him. He shook his head, snapping out of his trance. "Sorry, babe. What was that?"

"I said stick it in my cunt. I know that will make me cum." She smiled at him. "You want me to cum don't you?"

Marcus grinned. "Damn straight." Gently, he pulled the barrel out of her ass. Her asshole made a wet farting noise as the barrel popped out. They both giggled.

He aimed at her pussy, which seemed to glow wetly with anticipation. Slowly, he moved it closer.

Suddenly, Sophia grabbed the barrel. "No need to be so careful. You know my cunt can take the abuse!" And with that, she yanked on the gun, almost pulling it out of Marcus' hands.

Instantly, she jammed a good six inches of the steel barrel into herself. Marcus helped, enjoying himself immensely. He worked the barrel back and forth, using more of the barrel length than he had done with her asshole.

Soon, he was sliding in and out over 10 inches of length. The metal was slick with her cunt juice.

Sophia moaned, arching her back. She had let go of the barrel and gripped the bedsheets with intensity.

More and more Marcus fucked her with the shotgun, in and out over and over. Sophia's whole body now gyrated and shook with the rapturous act. Her pussy was making wet farting noises with every thrust and pull.

"Faster!" she cried.

"I am!" he said. And he was. So much so his arms were starting to get tired. He almost felt like a plumber trying to unclog a particularly difficult drain.

Then, Sophia gasped with near ecstasy.

"You okay, babe?" Marcus asked.

She seemed to be trying to catch her breath. Marcus grew concerned.

"Want me to stop?"

"Nooooooo!" she shouted at the ceiling. She started to finger her clit almost angrily.

"What?"

"Rack it!" she cried.

"What?"

"The shotgun! Rack a round into it! Now!"

Marcus obliged, although he was careful to make sure the safety was still on, and his finger was no where near the trigger. Hey, this was her kink, and he was happy to play along. Just didn't need to accidentally shoot her head off through her cunt.

The dark humour made him grin wider, and he racked a round into the chamber, keeping the barrel buried deep inside her hungry wet cunt. The shotgun made a loud CHUCK-CHUCK noise.

That movement sent Sophia over the edge as she furiously fingered her exposed clit. She bucked, and moaned wildly.

Marcus loved every second of it. "Fuck yeah, babe!" he said.

Her orgasm fading, Sophia reached down and grabbed the shotgun barrel. She guided in and out of herself, letting the feeling ease her arousal. Finally, after several long moments Marcus slid it out of her.

She gasped with pleasure, pinching her big curvy tits. The flesh around her pussy was sopping wet, and the flesh of her cunt was spread wide and a bright pink. Marcus bent down and gave her pussy a long sloppy kiss, slurping up some of its succulent juice.

"You're a wild child," he said, chin wet.

Still squeezing her tits and rubbing at her nipples she said, "You make me wild."

Marcus looked at the end of the shotgun barrel. It gleamed with her wetness. "I'm normally anal about keeping my guns clean since they're the main tool of our trade. But I'm not gonna this time. If I gotta pull the trigger on someone we'll think of it as pussy shots."

This made Sophia howl with laughter. *Fuck, Marcus was hot!* She thought to herself.

She crawled over to him and began to wrestle with his belt. The bulge in his jeans was prominent to the point of bursting through the fabric.

Marcus gently took her hands, stopping her. She pouted.

"I wanna suck you off, babe," she said, licking her lips with blatant hunger. "Suck your black barrel off until there isn't a drop left. I want all of that brown sugar!" She sounded almost like a crazed animal.

Marcus was about to agree when the alarm on his phone went off. "Shit," he said. "No time now. Got to keep on schedule." He gently pushed her away.

She agreed, but could not mask her disappointment. They were professionals after all. But even professionals could be allowed to have some fun.

Marcus put his game face on, suddenly serious. "Let's get going. We have an appointment with riches we can't miss."

Sophia quickly dressed as Marcus double checked their gear. She loved watching him when he was like this. Together, they were bad. Really really bad. And now they were going to do something that would prove to the world how bad they could be.

They carried their gear in tout bags out of their hotel room. People passed them by not realizing what was inside them. This gave Sophia a secret thrill.

As they walked towards Marcus' Mustang he could not help but notice Sophia was walking with a slight limp.

"Feeling a little sore this morning, miss?" He said with a knowing smile.

Sophia's smile matched his. "Yeah. Feel like a just got reamed raw by a shotgun. You'd limp, too."

Marcus laughed. "Don't go getting any more ideas now in that pretty head of yours."

She stuck her tongue out at him.

They threw the touts into the back seat and climbed into the front. Almost in unison they put sunglasses on.

"Couple of bad asses," Marcus said.

Sophia checked the time. "Hey! We're way ahead of schedule." She glared at him, thinking of how much more gun play she could have had back in the room.

"Know why?" Marcus asked as he started the Mustang. The engine rumbled to life like a living beast.

"Why?"

Marcus put it in drive. "Cause we're fucking professionals. That's why." He slammed on the gas. The Mustang surged forward across the parking lot. He peeled out onto the road.

They both laughed at the reactions of the people how gaped at them. Charged up with sex and an impending crime, they were ecstatic.

The hotel was only ten minutes distance from the bank, and Marcus got them there in three minutes. Soon, they turned onto the block with the bank up on the left hand side.

Sophia's heart was now pounding with excitement. Other than getting fucked by Marcus, nothing else was as thrilling as hitting a bank. They had done enough of them to settle on a comfortable, and safe routine.

Casually as can be, they drove past the bank. While Marcus watched the road, playing the dutiful driver, Sophia looked.

"Anything unusual?" he said as he turned down a side street. They would loop around to their waiting spot.

"Nothing," she said. "Noone inside yet."

"Perfect," Marcus said.

"No, you're perfect," she said, smiling.

"We're perfect little devils," he said as he smoothly pulled into a spot on the side of the road. From here they had the perfect vantage point of the front door, as well as anything along the side of the bank building. Just as they originally planned.

Now they just had to sit and wait.

The street was quiet, with only the occasional passerby in the distance.

Sophia gave Marcus a serious look. "You didn't let me suck you off back at the hotel."

"No time."

She motioned to the bank. "We got time. You promised I could have it. Why not a little fun while we wait."

Before Marcus could tell her no she said, "I'll stop as soon as he comes. Or you cum. Whoever *cums* first." She offered him a most enticing smile.

Marcus tried to argue the point but knew her hunger for his cock was insatiable. Besides, it *would* help ratchet down the tension he was feeling.

Sophia took his hesitation as a yes. She squealed with joy and shifter over to him in the seat. She fumbled with his belt buckle. "Got to let the beast out of its cage. Poor thing."

Marcus eased the driver's seat back a little as Sophia undid his belt and then his zipper. They both gave a quick look around. No one. Perfect.

She dug into his open pants and fished for his cock which flopped out. He was already partially erect.

“Fuck yeah,” Sophia said. She leaned in close to it. Marcus could feel her breath on his prick, her long dark hair caressing his exposed skin.

She started jerking at it. Turning her head to look up at him she said, “No time for foreplay, honey. Gonna make this quick but sweet.”

“Yeah,” Marcus said. He could feel his dick getting harder. Still, he managed to keep one eye on the front of the bank.

Sophia eased up a little on the tugging action, and slowly spit on his swollen prick. Not satisfied there was enough she spit even more. The top of his black cock was covered in her saliva, with one string of spittle extending from her bottom lip to the side of his shaft.

Like the fluttering wings of a butterfly, she flickered her tongue against his wet swollen prick. Several times she spit again, and even kissed the top of its head with pouted lips. She enjoyed the noise she made when she kissed his dick.

Suddenly, a man walked by their car.

Marcus, alarmed, grabbed the back of her head with one hand. Thinking he wanted her to swallow his cock, Sophia bent her head down, engulfing the entire length of his sizable dick with one motion.

Marcus gasped, tensing up. The man had sauntered by without even looking in their direction. He turned a corner and was gone.

Sophia gagged on his big dick. She had plunged it so its prick was now firmly lodged inside her throat several inches. But she was a trooper and held her head there. Her nose was jammed into the warm flesh of his left pelvis, and her lips were against the dark skin at the very base of his shaft.

The small trim forest of his pubic hair tickled her face. His testicles were now touching her right cheek.

Her mouth was *crammed* full, yet with amazing skill honed over the years of sucking many, many dicks, she managed to play her tongue around the ample shaft.

"Shiiiiiiit," Marcus moaned.

Sophia held herself there, feeling his throbbing cock deep inside her throat, and practically pushing against the back of her skull. She breathed through her nose, Marcus' pubic hair tickle her nostrils.

Then, after several long minutes, she slowly moved up his hard cock, slurping noisily the whole time.

She withdrew his dick, coughing and sputtering a little. His cock was absolutely slick with her spit, its prick glistening pleasantly in the morning sun.

Taking a few quick breathes, she then jammed it back into her mouth and up into her throat again. Then she withdrew. She did this over and over. Cock all in, cock all out.

Soon, she started to pick up speed. With a little adjustments to her technique she was in full suck mode.

Marcus was going practically cross eyed, holding the back of her head with one hand, the other on the steering wheel. He was mindful to not go near the car horn.

He really started to get into it as he felt the phantom tickle of an impending orgasm draw near. He grabbed her head with both hands and started to gyrate his hips while in his seat. His cock moved up and down into Sophia's welcoming hot mouth.

Faster and faster he thrust into her skull, like a piston on a race car about to blow out. Deep into her throat, he thrust. Sophia could feel his prick pummelling the back of it.

And she loved it.

The car was filled with the rapid sound of Sophia's wet continuous suction.

Then, it happened. Marcus moaned in pleasure, his body going tense.

From within her throat, Sophia felt his hot seed shoot into it. Marcus had stopped fucking her face as he came. She got a firm grip on his shaft and kept sucking. Her lips never lost their wet grip on his cock, ensuring every last sticky drop of his hot cum went right were it belonging. In her mouth.

Marcus let out another rapturous moan. Sophia had now managed to literally suck him dry. No more brown sugar to suck out of him.

Suddenly, Marcus sat upright.

"Shit!" Marcus hissed.

"What?"

"The bank manager. He's here!"

From his lap, Sophia peered out the front windshield. "Oh, crap. He's early. Way early." She looked at Marcus. "Does this mess things up? Can we still do it?" She sat up, wiping cum from her lips and licking them quickly.

Marcus put his wet dick back into his pants and did up his zipper. He offered his trademark evil-doers grin. "Honey," he said. "We can do *anything*."

They watched as the manager unlocked the door, oblivious to anyone who might be watching. Sophia made sure her face was clean of jizz in the side view mirror. She coughed up a little burp, the kind given after a good meal.

Marcus chuckled. "Like a pig in a poke."

A couple of women, bank tellers arrived, too. The manager let them in, and followed after.

Sophia was eager. "Did he leave the door unlocked again?"

"Yup," said Marcus. "Just like every morning for the last two weeks."

Sophia laughed.

"Let's do this," Marcus said. They leaned into each other and kissed passionately. Their tongues seeking each other out with a wild hunger.

Then they got out of the Mustang, and grabbed their bags. From those they took out a pair of long coats and put them on. Then, with a quick glance around to see if there was no one else looking, they withdrew their shotguns, and hide them under their coats.

They walked purposefully towards the bank door. Looking up and down the street, checking again, they then withdrew full masks. Devil's Heads masks, complete with little horns. His was red, hers was blue.

"Don't need these masks to know how bad we are, baby." Marcus said as he pulled his on.

When Sophia did the same, they nodded at each other and went inside.

Sophia locked the door behind them.

Marcus was already striding across the bank which, because they planned it that way, was empty of customers. The tellers were over at a coffee machine, contemplating its slow percolation.

"Down on the floor, NOW!" he shouted.

The tellers looked at him in shock. The manager came running out of his office, a half eaten doughnut in his hand.

Marcus fired into the ceiling. The noise was deafening. "I said now!"

All three of them dropped to the ground.

Sophia had taken several steps into the bank to cover him, but her main job was to watch for other employees arriving. She would drag them in until the job was finished.

That was to be her focus. This was a serious situation after all.

Yet, standing there with his shotgun pointed at the tellers Sophia could not help but marvel at Marcus.

Up on the teller's counter, screaming hellfire at anyone who didn't move quick enough, he looked absolutely gorgeous. A sleek, well defined, tattooed god.

And just a few minutes earlier, her mouth was full of his fat cock, his cum spilling down her throat. She grinned.

Marcus threw an empty tout bag at the manager. "Fill it! Fast!"

The manager hasten to do as he was told. Sophia could see him stuffing huge handfuls of cash into the bag from the tellers counter.

Money! Money! Money!

Marcus made one of the tellers fill another bag.

He looked over at Sophia who checked outside for the thirtieth time, then nodded at him.

Marcus grabbed the full bag from the manager and told him to get on the ground. Then he did the same with teller.

He backed up towards Sophia, all the while watching the others cowering on the floor. He passed a bag over to Sophia. Its weight was orgasmic!

"Stay down, or we'll come back and massacre you all!" He shouted with menace.

Sophia unlocked the door and stepped outside. Marcus followed. Amazingly, the street was quiet. Still too early. Luck was on there side.

They hustled towards the Mustang. They didn't want it in front of the bank in case it created a drama for being parked there.

Sophia was absolutely charged up. "We did it!"

Marcus was all business. "Not yet. We still gotta..."

Just then they heard sirens. Lots of them. And close by.

"Oh, shit!" he said. "Move!"

They ran to the Mustang, threw the full bags in the backseat, and quickly got inside. Sophia hung onto her shotgun, eyes scanning around.

Marcus started the car with a loud revving, and they quickly sped off.

About three blocks away Sophia looked back. As Marcus turned a corner she caught the glimpse of a black and white cop car, lights flashing, sirens blaring, race past. It was headed towards the bank.

She let out a relieved sigh. "They're not following us."

Marcus was concentrating on the road. "Not yet. They will be soon enough if we don't get to the warehouse now."

Once they were a further distance away from the bank and the noise of sirens, Marcus slowed down a little so as not to be pulled over for speeding.

Soon, they were in the warehouse district. They had scouted this place out beforehand, thoroughly, and knew exactly where to go. Into an abandoned section was a run down and empty warehouse building.

Marcus pulled up to its loading dock door. Sophia got out. While she rolled the door up, Marcus drove the Mustang around, and skillfully backed in through the door. Sophia pulled the door down.

He parked the Mustang in the middle the wide empty warehouse. The engine noise echoing throughout. He killed it and got out. Sophia ran over to him.

"We did it, babe!" she shouted as she leaped into his arms for a big hug.

They kissed passionately, tongues going deep into the other's mouth.

"Now what?" she asked.

"Now we stick to the plan. We wait."

She pouted at him, playing it up. "That's gonna be a while. Hiding out here until things cool down." She pressed her hand up against his crotch. "While things cool down out there, they can heat up in here. Got to pass the time somehow."

Marcus laughed. "Okay, babe. You convinced me." He knew they would not be bothered here and could hideout here for days if necessary.

Delighted, Sophia stepped back from him and peeled off her shirt. Her large wonderful breasts flopped out enticingly. Then went the pants and panties. Soon she was buck naked in front of him, her tattoo prominent across her breast. Her sensual curves made him drool.

"You next," she demanded.

Marcus obliged, and quickly followed suite. He felt a little silly standing naked in the cool empty warehouse, big black cock in his hand.

"Well, we got time," he looked at her meaningfully. "So lets make it count. Where you want to do it? On the hood? In the back seat?" He smiled. "On the roof?"

She shook her head. "Nope. I got a better idea. Something we've never done before."

Naked, big tits jiggling, she walked over to the Mustang, Sophia leaned into it and pulled out one of the tout bags. She grinned wickedly at him. Then, she upturned the bag, and wads of cash spilt out onto the concrete floor.

"What are you doing?" Marcus said, incredulous.

Sophia reached into the Mustang again. This time she pulled out a shotgun. She pointed it at him.

Eyes wide, cautioning hands in the air, Marcus said, "Babe? What the hell?"

She gave him a serious look now. "I want to fuck on a bed of money!" She racked a round into the shotgun. CHUCK-CHUCK! "Now get you black ass down on the ground. I'm gonna ride you long and hard!"

Marcus chuckled. *Fuckin Wild Child!*

Still naked, he did as he was told. He lay down on the cold floor, cash in their bank wrappers pressing against his skin.

Sophia smiled and sauntered over, her beautiful curvy naked form was actually made all the more sexier by the shotgun in her hands. She spread her legs on either side of him as she moved forward until she stood over his crotch.

Her hot pussy presented itself to him. For a moment, Marcus was happily overwhelmed but the dominance she had over him.

Slowly, Sophia squatted down, shotgun in both hands pointed at the ceiling.

For a moment they heard the faint sound of a distant siren. They both paused. It faded away. She smiled back down at him. Squatting over him, she slide her pussy back and forth against the long length of his black penis.

"Put it in me," she commanded.

Marcus used a hand and pointed his fat dick upwards. Sophia eased down on it, until she enveloped him completely. Slowly she rocked her hips forward and back, all the while still holding the shotgun. She was incredibly wet. Turned on by the crime they just committed. Turned on by the pursuing cops.

Turned on by *him.*

Faster and faster she gyrated, perfect tits jiggling, the shotgun pressed against them. Occasionally she bounced up and down, the wet smacking noise of their flesh hitting each other filling the empty warehouse.

Again, there was the faint sound of sirens, but neither one of the them gave it any notice.

Marcus played with her big tits, squeezing them, pinching her nipples. She moved the shotgun away from herself slightly so he could do so. She looked down on him with hooded eyes.

Soon in became to much for Marcus; her succulent body grinding his cock, bouncing on him. The movement of her tits. Her excited breathing. The robbery. The sound of sirens.

Sophia did not let up, grinding with full force against him, feeling his big cock flop around insider her. She actually growled with the intensity.

Marcus came. He bucked wildly, hands digging into her ample hips harder as she still moved against him. Soon he was completely spent. He gasped with pleasure.

"Fuuuuuuck...." he said. He had a goofy grin plastered on his face.

Sophia leaned down and kissed him, sweaty tits pressing against his sweaty chest.

"Know what, baby?" Sophia said.

"No, tell me. I like to be informed." Marcus was starting to feel a little exhausted from the day's activities.

"Post-robbery sex is the *best*!" Sophia declared.

They laughed.

"Who the *hell* are you people?" Someone shouted.

They both looked over in shock.

A security guard was standing over in a doorway. He looked at them, their naked bodies, the Mustang, and all the money spread around.

There was a very long moment when everyone tried to decide what to do.

The guard made the first move, and grabbed for his holstered gun.

Sophia reacted. Still straddling Marcus, his dick inside her, she pointed her shotgun as the guard fumbled his pistol out of its holster.

He drew on her. Sophia fired. The guard pinwheeled threw the air and slumped to the ground.

They heard shouting right next to the warehouse. In a distant window, they saw cops running past outside.

"Shit!" Marcus said.

They jumped up, raced to put there clothes on.

Sophia was aghast at what just happened. "I.... I had to!" she said, pulling her shirt back on over her big sweaty breasts.

Marcus pulled on his pants quickly, jamming his large cock into them. "I know! I know!" They started scooping up the money and just flinging it into the open car. The sirens outside were a lot louder. More shouting.

"Get in!" he said as he jumped behind the wheel. Sophia did too, slamming the door. She clung to the shotgun.

Just then, two cops entered the large room. They looked down at the dead body of the guard.

Sophia shouted, "Go!"

Marcus started the Mustang, jamming it into drive. The cops drew their weapons, pointed it at them. Marcus pulled away.

Sophia found herself shooting at them with the shotgun through the back windshield, shattering it.

"Hang on!" Marcus cried.

The Mustang crashed through the garage door with an incredible noise. Metal shrieking against metal. The windshield cracked. They were both jarred around by the impact. But they made it through.

To their horror, they saw cops and cop cars everywhere.

Marcus sped past them. There was shouting and gunfire. Bullets pinged off the car's metal. He drove out of the warehouse district with lightening speed and out into the main street. He headed towards an intersection.

Like a scene straight out of a movie, a black and white cop car zoomed around a corner and into the intersection, skidding sideways. Marcus roared and wrenched on the steering wheel.

The two vehicles smashed up beside each other. The cop car spun out and was left behind.

There were no more cop cars in the immediate area, but they could sure hear more. Marcus charged the Mustang ahead, unsure of where to go.

"Time for the shortcut outta here," Marcus said.

With that he spun in behind a factory, out of its back parking lot, and up along a gravel road into the woods. The sound of sirens grew more distant around them.

Sophia, eyes wide, looked at him in amazement. "You never told me about this shortcut?"

Marcus grinned. "Babe, I gotta have *some* secrets."

They both laughed as they drove off through the back roads, the sounds of pursuit growing more, and more distant.

END

Spanked Raw (Going Raw)

Antone loved books almost as much as he loved sex. Almost.

Yet, he never thought the two would actually collide together until he met the cute new employee at the book store.

He had been going to that store for many years. Occasionally, there would be an attractive clerk working there. Usually, it was someone who primarily stocked shelves with all the new releases. The work itself required lots of kneeling, stretching and bending.

When one of these cuties worked in his area, he found that sitting in one of the lounge chairs gave him a good view of their comings and goings. He loved the ones with curves. Big and beautiful. That's what turns him on the most.

Sadly, though, there seemed to be a high turnaround at the store. Whether to internal staff politics, general attrition (he couldn't imagine doing that type of work for years) or they here migrated to other branches, he never knew. But many hot, and/or cute, (or both) shelf stockers simply vanished from his almost weekly appreciations.

Or maybe they left because of him? He'd often wondered how obvious he was when he sneaked glances at their bums as the sauntered past, or bent down to add some books (That was certainly his favourite part of their job!). Also, as they were lost in the mundane concentration of their work, the almost never realized he was staring at their breasts. Side boob view was another favourite. You may not get a full appreciation of breasts full on, masked by a sweater or baggy blouse. But turned to the side, the breast was particularly arousing.

Antone was sure there was gossip amongst the female staff about the tall, handsome black man who drools over their every move. Or maybe he was just thinking to much of himself?

He had found himself going to the store more and more ever since things went south with his long time girlfriend, Lydia. She was curvy as the got, and the sex was always fantastic. But she had just admitted to him that she had started seeing a coworker of hers, and their relationship was pretty much over and done with.

This put Antone in the dumps, and he eventually sought solace in the books at the store.

Then one day, there was a new short brunette clerk working there. She was about his age, and wonderfully curvy in all the ways he liked. A real knockout. Thankfully, a lot of her books needed stocking right in front of where he was sitting and he nearly lost his mind each time she bent over. Her round ass was to die for.

Playing casual, he peeked at her from over the edge of his book, thus allowing him to ogle her magnificent butt. *Jeans were created to be worn by this girl*, he thought.

She had bent over, revealing the beautiful roundness of her ass.

He felt himself getting hard, and he looked down at his crotch, making sure everything was still in order and not bulging out at a revealing angle.

"Found what you are looking for?" asked a pleasant female voice.

He looked up, and blanched. It was her. The brunette cutie was standing directly in front of him.

What did she mean? Looking for my boner? A book? Her?

"Uh," was all he could manage in that moment of shock. He became frighteningly aware of bulge growing bigger.

Did her eyes just flicker down at it? He thought, embarrassed. Maybe was she just looking at the book in his hand?

"Enjoying the selection?" she asked, with a crook of her eyebrow. Her expression seemed to show more than a passing interest in what his answer could be.

Was she flirting with him?

"Yeah, great selection. Thanks," Antone said. *Geez, could I sound more stupid?*

"I'm Cora," she suddenly offered. "Just started here today."

He was a little tongue tied, not expecting to have to actually *interact* with this object of desire. *Who'd of thunk of such a concept?*

"Antone," he said. His heart was now thundering against his chest. Hopefully, his face didn't go red like it usually did when he was flustered.

"Well, Antone," Cora said with a smile and a wink. "Maybe I'll see you around?"

"Yeah, definitely," he said.

She turned to go, but paused. His heart stopped.

She nodded her head at his... crotch? At his growing hard on? He wanted to cross his legs but his erection would just make it look even funnier.

"By the way, you're reading it upside down," she grinned wickedly at him, and walked away, pushing the cart. He could have sworn she put in an extra bit of sway to those perfect hips.

He watched her leave, a bit in a daze. Looking at the book in his hands, he saw that she was right.

Stunned, he waited for his hard on to die down. He even managed to read a little of the book (right side up this time), until he felt he had embarrassed himself enough for one day.

He was walking towards the exit when he suddenly heard something.

"Antone!" someone hissed from behind. He turned and was struck dumb when he saw that it was Cora. She was leaning around the end of a bookshelf, out of sight of the front door cash register. She peeked down towards the cashier then, looking back at him, waved his hand at him, indicating he should come over.

Thankfully, his legs took the initiative and propelled him to her, before his brain could screw things up.

When he got close, and obviously wasn't moving fast enough for her, she grabbed his arm and pulled him behind the shelves. Her firm touch electrified his bare skin. He found himself grinning.

She grinned back. "Got a question for you, Antone." she said, looking quite beautiful.

"Okay," was all he could say.

"Wanna fuck my brains out?"

His breath caught.

Oh.

My.

God.

His brain had seized up. Miraculously, he found himself nodding.

Pleased, she took his hand and quickly led him into a back storage room, which was filled with books, and boxes, from top to bottom. She closed the door behind them.

"Now, you're going to have to wait her until closing and everyone else leaves." She looked up at him with big wide stunning eyes that melted his heart and began to stiffen his crotch again. "Will you wait here for me, Antone?"

Duh.

Shrugging, he said, "Yeah, no problem, he said, casually. Like getting propositioned by store clerks was an everyday occurrence for him.

She nodded, but looked at him as if analyzing his honesty. "You know what?" she said.

"What?"

"Let me give you a little taste of what you can expect if you do stay."

Before he could say anything she dropped to her knees in front of him. His eyes widened, and his boner screamed to be released.

"Whip that black cock of your's out," she demanded.

There is a God! his brain seemed to cheer at him.

"Hurry," she said. "I'm only suppose to be on my coffee break." She looked up at him. "And I wanna little taste, too."

He had never unbuckled his belt, and undid his zipper, that fast before in his life. His erect dick practically popped out at her with the sudden motion of pulling down his pants past his waist.

She giggled a little, but immediately grabbed it. The warmth of her hand on his throbbing member, nearly made him cum right there, but he grit his teeth.

"Mmmm," she said. She very gently kissed the tip of his dick. "I like the taste of that. Gonna get me some of that brown sugar." She stuck out her tongue and flickered it against his swollen prick. She did this for several moments, alternating between kissing and flickering at it.

Then, suddenly, she opened her mouth wide and lunged forward. Nearly his entire cock was swallowed in one motion. He felt the top of his big cock slide against the roof of her mouth, and lodge in the back of her hot throat.

Antone moaned.

"Mmmm," she said again. At least that's what it sounded like. She did have a big cock in her mouth, after all.

Clinching her lips around his girth, she began to move her head up and down. She sucked at him, gently.

Soon, the only thing he could feel was her determined grip at the base of his shaft and part of her palm against his balls, and the hot sensation of the wonderful wet friction of his member sliding in and out of her mouth.

He moaned again. He was now having a heck of a time not cumming and preventing hot jizz from exploding out of the back of her head.

"Cora to the front cash! Cora to the front cash!" suddenly said a loud voice.

They both froze.

It was the intercom.

But she didn't lose her cool. Slowly, almost deliberately, she slide up his shaft, which now was slick with her spittle. Her sucking lips slide over his prick, but remained locked on the very tip of it. As she looked up at him he felt her tongue flicker feather-like at the tip.

Then she pulled it out and gave it one last quick kiss. She stood, and he found himself standing in front of her holding his wet throbbing dick. *Was it over?*

"This is not over," she said, as if reading his thoughts. She stood on her tip toes and kissed him on the lips.

"I liked that taste, and I'll be back for more," she said. "Think you can wait for me?" She grinned evilly.

"Yeah!" he gasped. *Sweet Lord Almighty, Yes!*

"Keep that black motor running," she said. And with that, she slipped out the door, and closed it behind her, locking it.

He was left standing there, pants down to his knees, holding his big dick.

Not wanting to rub one out (gotta save that for later), he did up his pants, and spent the time reading while waiting.

It didn't take long. Soon, some of the lights went off, but a bank of them stayed on in the storage room. Closing time.

Then, after what seemed like forever, the door clicked open, and for a brief moment, he thought someone other than Cora was going to come in and find him there.

It wasn't. Face beaming, Cora entered, and relocked the door behind her.

"Well, well, well," she said. "Tired of waiting?"

He sprang to his feet from the chair he had been reading in. "Nope, not at all. Uh, are we alone now?"

She smiled. "Yes, and let me prove it." Suddenly, in one fluid motion, she pulled off her shirt. Antone was rendered speechless, as she was not wearing a bra (which he had suspected), and her large breasts flopped out with the motion to present themselves to the world to be admired.

"Wow," he said. *God, those are a fantastic pair she's got!*

"It gets better," with a couple of quick motions, she pulled down her jeans, as well as her panties, down to her ankles. She grinned at him as she kicked off her shoes, and stepped out of everything. Curves everywhere. Big, wonderful curves!

Eager to join in the festivities, Antone quickly pulled off his own shirt, and tossed it. Then he started on his pants, before she walked over to him, and put her hands on his belt buckle. His eyes were on the trim triangle of hair that peeked out from between her thighs.

"Wait, not yet," she said.

Certain he would do as she asked, she sashayed over to the desk. Antone' eyes were locked on that amazingly round ass, and the pussy it promised.

She glanced back at him, then bent straight over the desk, so her elbows were leaning on it. Her huge breasts pooled beneath her. Wiggling her big ass, Antone could now see the well shaved pinkness of her pussy. "I want you to spank me," she said.

Transfixed by the movement of her naked flesh and that wondrous ass, he walked up behind her. Impulsively, he cupped her ample buttocks. *Sweet Nirvana!* He thought.

He wanted to fuck her so hard, right then and there, but decided to play along. Holding up a hand at the ready, he looked at her for his cue.

"Spank me," she said. So he did, with a light slap. First one cheek, and then the other. He really enjoyed how her large beautiful buttocks moved when he did so.

She shuddered, and said, "Harder! And don't be a pussy about it!"

Well, okay then, he thought.

He did, this time a little harder, and using his full palm, not just the fingers. She yelped, and he found his hand actually stung.

"More!"

"Yes, Ma'am!" he said, and did so. Over and over he smacked her lovely ass, until it progressed to a full on spanking. Each time she yelped, or groaned. She even gritted her teeth to keep from screaming out, but that didn't last long as he kept at it. Smack, smack, smack.

She raised a hand. "Okay, okay," she panted. "Stop!"

Disappointed, he did. "Did I hurt you?" He hadn't wanted to have this kinky little exercise end due to him being overzealous.

"No," she said. "Not yet." She grinned evilly.

Antone nearly cam in his pants from her expression alone.

"Not yet?" he echoed, oblivious to the meaning, but wanting to know more, all the same.

She pointed to one of the carts, which was full of thick hardcovers. "Grab a classic."

Obeying, he walked over to it, feeling his hard-on chaff roughly against the inside of his pants. Not trying to be subtle, he shifted his dick over with one hand, as he picked out a book from the cart selection with the other.

"How about this?" he asked.

Her panting had lessened, and she was using a hand to reach around and massage her the bright red skin of her ass. "Is it a classic?"

"Classic?" he looked. "Uh, it's about medicine or something."

She had moved a finger over her raw pussy, and she flinched with ecstasy at the painful touch. "No, not that one. Get something good, something that has meaning."

Confused at the request, but not wanting to question it for fear of putting a sudden end to this wonderful encounter, he picked out another book.

"The Complete Dickens Collection," he said hefting the large tome. It was thick and weight a good couple pounds.

She nodded with a smile, one finger teasing the wetness of her pussy around. "That will do. It has Dick in it."

Antone actually laughed out loud. She laughed too.

He was not going to argue this, so he stood behind her, and to one side. *Fuck she looks hot*, he thought. She had braced her arms on the desk again, big boobs dangling pendulous, in preparation of the wonderful pain.

He gripped the big book with both hands, and hoisted it over one shoulder. This view accentuated the wonder curve of her buttock muscles, and again, his boner begged to be released.

"I'd really like to fuck the hell out you right now," he admitted. He almost regretted blurting it out, but God damn this chick looked fuckable as all hell.

She winked at him over shoulder, "Soon. Very soon you can cram that massive black dick of yours inside me, I promise. But first, do this to me. I need it to get going." She smiled.

God, I am one lucky guy, he thought. His face actually hurt from grinning so much.

"Ready?" he asked.

Without saying anything, she faced forward again, and nodded her head vigorously. She was psyching herself up.

Cora took a deep breath. He took a deep breath.

Antone swung hard aiming at the underside curve of her ass.

She grunted, but gritted her teeth. And he smacked her again, then again. Over and over.

At first, she kept the noise she made to a minimum, but as he kept spanking her with the big book, she started to get louder. Soon, she was almost shouting with each and every smack.

Her body would even quiver with the anticipation of each hit. But she didn't tell him to stop. She only flinched, making her huge tits jiggle.

Eventually, she raised her hand again, and he stopped. She was breathing too hard from the shrieking to say anything at first. He lowered the book, and waited. His cock throbbed in his pants for her. She looked so damned fuckable.

"Okay, okay!" she was gasping. "Now get some Shakespeare!"

Was she kidding? When were they gonna fuck? He thought, incredulous. But he did as he was asked. When a hot, naked chick, who is bent over begging to be spanked and spanked hard, asks you to do something that turns her on even more; you did it, damn it!

He got it, and it was twice the size of the other. His eyes widened as he hefted it. "Are you sure?" he asked, concerned.

"Yeah," she said, nodding quickly. "Do it now before I change my mind! Spank my ass with it!"

Again, he smacked her, again she shrieked with pain and delight. He repeated this over and over until he was certain the bright red skin on her ass was going to burst from all that punishment.

This time, she did not last as long as previously before she raised her hand, and he stopped.

He found his fingers actually started to hurt, where they got caught between the book and the firm flesh of her ass. He could even see they made a couple of impressions on her lovely skin. Red on red.

She was gasping for air, and her whole body quivered and shook. *Is she having an orgasm?* He thought.

"Okay," she said, gulping in air. "Pants off! Black cock out!"

He did not require any further coaxing, and his shoes, pants and boxers flew in different directions within seconds.

Bent over as she was, her pussy was pushed out, glistening. He could see she was very wet, to the point where it dribbled all down her lips, and partially down one of her inner thighs.

His mouth watered just looking at it.

"Eat me," she said. "Lick me all up."

All right! He got down on his knees, lightly gripped her red ass, spreading the big round cheeks a little. Then he licked her; nice and long at first, from the bottom to the top. *Or was it top to the bottom from this angle?* he thought.

She tasted incredible and he told her so. Her pussy was sopping wet from being turned on so much from the spanking. He could feel the heat of the blood brought so close to the surface of her red skin, rubbing against his cheeks and chin. He licked her for several long tasty minutes until she was moaning again. He could feel her wetness all over his chin, and some dribbled a little down his throat.

Careful, he sucked out her clit between his lips, and it was his turn to use his tongue for flickering.

Cora arched her back, groaning. Occasionally she pushed back so his face was forced deeper inside her incredible wetness, and he nearly went mad with the feeling of it.

He worked on her pussy like this for a long time, sucking up her lips so their soft folds slipped in gently between his teeth. Her entire body shuddered and quaked. Eventually, she couldn't handle any more, and said, "Fuck me!"

She looked over her shoulder at his eyes that peeked over the curvature of her ass. "Fuck me with your Dickens!"

He stood up, grabbed his dick (or was it Dickens?) which was now throbbing, and put his other hand on her ass. Then, very slowly, he slide his prick into her. He bite his bottom lip because he nearly lost it right there.

Taking a moment to gather himself, he then slid his entire length into her. He gasped. She felt so damn good; very hot, and very wet. Then he slid back his length until it was nearly out, and slammed it back in all the way. She grunted. He did it again. And again.

Antone pumped her, as hard as she had asked him to. He marvelled at the the bright redness of her ass, and gazed down appreciatively at her little pink ass-hole. He rubbed at her asshole with a thumb, all the while not stopping with his rhythm. Her flesh jiggled provocatively from his efforts.

Cora tossed her head back and forth, occasionally arching her back all the way so he could reach around and squeeze her big tits. At one point he pulled her back by the elbows so she was almost standing up straight, and slammed her pussy harder and harder.

Soon, after all that had happened, and with the incredible sensation of being finally inside her, he couldn't hold it any longer.

"Ah, fuck!" Antone groaned loudly.

She instinctively knew what this meant, reached back and gently pushed at his stomach so he eased out of her. Her pussy made wet noises as if in protest.

Spinning around, she dropped to her knees in front of him, and as he stroked his long shaft, she slurped his dick into her hot mouth. She sucked furiously until he practically screamed as he finally exploded into her mouth.

Somehow she managed to chuckle while sucking him off. His hips bucked with his orgasm, as if he was fucking her mouth. When he was nearly spent, she swallowed loudly, never letting his cock out of her mouth. He sagged against the desk as she continued to nurse his load.

"Whoa," he said. He could feel his body was covered in sweat from such wonderful exertion.

She pulled his cock out of her mouth with a wet pop, and said, "Well, Antone. Thanks for the brown sugar. Your big black dick really topped off my day." She smiled and returned to sucking him dry.

Chuckling, Antone couldn't agree more!

END

Wet & Raw (Going Raw)

Avery faced a long, and boring drive through the countryside as she headed south to visit family for the holidays.

She found the radio annoying as it continuously played sappy love songs over and over, so she just turned off. Unfortunately, this left her with her thoughts and memories of her failing relationship with her husband, Kyle. They had been married for less than three years but she knew it was doomed from the beginning.

He even made the occasion comment about her weight which she simply brushed off. I'm big and beautiful! That's what you married, asshole. Needless to say, the passion that initially attracted them to each other faded quickly and they simply fell into the routine of having each other around.

And it was passion she wanted more of in her life, and since there was no more with Kyle she made the painful decision of eventually cancelling the whole thing. Despite the feelings of it being amicable, the whole situation was still quite stressful.

The early morning sun gave an orange hew to the sky, and tinged the countless trees that strobe by her on both sides of the winding country road. There was very little traffic, which was why she purposely took this more scenic route to her parents house several states away. She did not mind peacefulness but having Kyle around for so many years she found a lack of another person's presence daunting.

She had no one else in her life at the moment to fill the void. Neither she nor Kyle were unfaithful to the other during their failing relationship. And having only just decided to separate she had neither the time, nor the will, to find someone else.

What she really craved with someone to find her. A distraction of the momentary kind. She did not think she had the emotional toolkit to deal with anything too heavy.

"I just need a man," she said to herself. "I man who will love my curves as much as I do." She laughed at the absurdity of that declaration. She wasn't gonna find anyone at her parent's house, that was for certain. And she sure as hell didn't think anyone was waiting for her out here, in the middle of nowhere.

She peered up at the mountains, each covered with an apron of thick forest, that she slowly past by. "Nope," she said. "Only thing out here are mountain men and Bigfoot. And both would be too smelly for my taste."

As her mind wandered, she concentrated less on the road. At a particularly sharp turn, a figure suddenly appeared directly in front of her. A *man*, standing dangerously close to the edge of the turn in the road.

She yelped, and yanked at the wheel, swerving to avoid him. Her car fish tailed and she fought to control it. Pumping the brakes she managed to avoid flying off the road and into the trees. Always a cautious driver, she had not been travelling too fast and she skidded to a stop directly on the meridian facing the direction she had been coming from.

Her fingers were dug into the steering wheel and her hair was now in her face, which puffed out as she breathed heavily.

Is that what it's like to almost die?, she thought. She barked out a laugh, still in shock.

It was only after a few moments of recovering that Avery realized someone was running towards the car. The stupid guy!

Oh, I'm going to tear a strip out of him! she thought as she released her vice like grip from the steering wheel, and pushed back her hair.

Her eyes widened in surprise as he got closer. *Sweet Lord,* she thought. The man who approached was tall, dark and handsome. And beautifully black. *This guy looks like one of those underwear models you see on bus shelter poster ads. What the heck was he doing way out here?*

Avery found the wherewithal to roll down the window as he ran up to her driver's side door. His stunningly handsome face was only slightly marred by his expression of concern.

"What's an underwear model doing way out here?" she blurted. She put her hand to her mouth and she gasped at her own stupidity. "Was that my outside voice?"

He didn't seem to hear her, and said, "Are you all right? Are you hurt at all?" His voice was deep and husky. His light jacket emphasized his wide shoulders, and his jeans did little to hide his muscular thighs. For some bizarre reason his body reminded her of the trees all around, tall and strong.

Like a mountain man's!

"Yes," Avery finally managed to say. "I think I'm alive." She grinned up at him.

He sagged with relief, smiling for the first time, and she found his perfect teeth out did the brightness of the morning sun. His dark skin was sheened with a light sweat from walking outside in the warm weather. Avery found herself wanting me *make* this ebony man-god sweat for a different reason.

"Well, that's relief," he said, placing his hands on the rolled down window. She could not help but notice they were large and strong looking.

She caught herself wondering just how gentle those strong hands could be, moving up and down her body.

"I am so sorry," he said. "It was my fault. I didn't realize I was so close to the road. My car broke down." He hitched a thumb over at the little dodge parked on the road side.

"Oh, no, it was my fault," she said. "I wasn't paying attention, my thoughts drifted..." and as she said that she realized her drifting thoughts had been about a much needed man to distract her from her troubles. She looked up at his handsome face, with its chiseled features and strong jaw. *And I go ahead and nearly kill the only man for miles!*

"I can't get any reception on my phone," he said. "Could I use yours to call for a tow truck?"

"Sorry, but I don't have one," she said, sheepishly.

"Ah, that's too bad," he said, disappointed. He was looking at her, smiling, when she had a thunderous revelation.

"Hey," Avery said sweetly. "Since I almost splattered you all over the road, the least I could do is offer you a ride." She felt her face reddening as she spoke, trying not make it obvious what kind of ride she really had in mind. *There are curves out here, other than on the road.*

He arched a brow, considering the offer. She marvelled at his gorgeous brown eyes. She could lose herself in them forever. If he let her.

Finally, he said, "Where are you headed?"

"South. A long way south, actually."

He frowned a little and Avery was momentarily mortified she would lose him. But again, he regarded her with that sexy arch of the eyebrow. "I think the next town is only a couple of miles further up the road." He shrugged as if to suggest he really didn't want to bother her any more.

Oh, he could bother her, alright. Bother her in several ways, and in several different positions, too.

Avery grinned. "I'll take you. It's the least I could do. It might keep me from running you over again when I turn around."

He laughed. "Okay. You win. Just let me grab my stuff." He trotted back to his car.

She watched the movement of his buttocks in his jeans as he moved.

Yum, yum, yum, Avery thought. She envisioned those buttocks clenching tightly as he thrust his length deep into her. *Hot damn, I've bagged myself a handsome sexy black man!*

She turned the car around in a wide arch, to point back in the southerly direction she was original travelling. This time she didn't almost kill him.

Avery watched as he grabbed a duffel bag from the front seat, then locked the car. Her heart was pounding excitedly in her chest and threatened to burst out from between her ample bosom. She looked at herself in the rear view mirror, and made a vain attempt at fixing her tussled hair. She locked eyes with herself.

Do you know what you are doing girl?

She grinned. *Yes, I'm going to be doing him! Lick some dark chocolate all over!*

He came back, and threw his bag in the backseat. Then he sat down in the passenger side, closing the door. As he settled in, Avery sneaked a peak at his crotch, which bulged prominently.

Yup, she thought, *he definitely has a penis*. With that confirmed, she now made it her mission to find out if he knew how to use it. If not, she sure as hell would have fun teaching him.

He turned and smiled at her, offering his big hand.

"I'm Tyreese."

She took it, and tried not to shiver with the electric touch of him. His palm was callused, and she pictured it moving smoothly over her naked curvy skin.

"Avery, nice to... uh... almost run into you."

They shook and chuckled.

Avery found she was unwilling to release his hand right away. But when Tyreese arched that brow again and added that cute smile, she relented. She pulled out on the road and drove, trying mightily to keep her eyes from staring at him.

They made very idle chit chat, of which none involved her getting naked, and him spanking her, or her smothering him with large sweaty breasts. She was just trying to work up the courage to make it happen. Yet, she got the distinct sense he was intrigued by her. Maybe even found her attractive.

It only took a few minutes but they arrived at the town turnoff. Avery's mind was racing. She had an impulse and by God she was going to see it through, this time! She slowed the car.

"Hey, what's that over there," Avery said pointing towards what looked like the entrance to an old dirt road that disappeared into the forest.

Tyreese looked. "Looks like a switchback road," he said. "Runaway truck use them in an emergency."

"Wow. I've never seen one of those maybe I'll go down a little ways just to check out. Would be nice and private." Avery looked at him meaningfully. "Care to come have an emergency with me, Tyreese?"

His eyebrows had raised in surprise making him look all the more adorable.

A second passed and then another, each feeling like years to Avery.

Tyreese chuckled slightly, then settled back in his seat. He then regarded her with a seductive smile. "That's a fantastic idea," he said.

Avery laughed.

Hoping not to lose him in the moment, she quickly steered the car onto the switchback road.

She drove slowly down the gravel road while fully conscious of the glances he was giving her. The moment the highway seemed a safe distance out of view, she pulled over as far as she could and parked, again.

She turned the car off, and killed the power, too, and sat back.

They both grinned nervously at each other.

"Well," Avery said. "What do we do now?"

Tyreese made a show of looking around at their surroundings. "I dunno. Is this the spot you normally take the men you almost run over?"

She laughed, undid her seat belt, and moved over to him closing the distance. Placing a hand on his strong shoulder she whispered in his ear, "Yes, and I would like to suck your black cock, as an apology." To ensure he did not miss her meaning, she grabbed the bulge in his jeans. She was happy to note that it was already growing in size.

"Yes, ma'am!" Tyreese said, and leaned back to undo his belt. She helped him. When it was undone he eased his hips forward so she would have room.

Avery fished his dick out of its hiding place, it was firm and erect. A growing, dark anaconda of lust. She kissed the tip of his fat prick several times, feeling its throbbing heat in her hand. Gently, she started to lick its length, up and down from the base of his shaft to the swollen prick. Like a lollipop.

He gasped softly, putting one hand on the back of her head to guide her up and down movements.

Tyreese then reached down, found the release for the chair and angled it back some more, giving her more room to work on him properly. She happily settled in to get to work on him, good and proper.

With his knob glistening from her diligent licking, Avery then took his fat prick into her mouth, pushing it up to the back of her throat as far as it would go. Her lips firmly gripped his shaft as they moved closer to the base, her nose touched his stomach. Then she sucked at it, moving her head up and down all the way. She stroked him with her hand, following it with her lips.

Tyreese groaned.

For several long wonderful minutes she sucked his big cock, until he reached a point she was certain he was going to shoot his load. The car filled with sound of her hard sucking, and hungry slurping. Occasionally, a vehicle passed by on the highway. Neither one them gave a damn.

Carefully, Avery slowed, not wanting him to be spent too soon. Kissing the tip of his prick on more time, she then looked up at him with a big smile.

She said, “Let's fuck now, okay?”

Tyreese smiled back, but offered that cute arching brow again. “It's a little crowded in here for that, don't you think?”

She sat up a little and said, "Well, you are a big boy. Let's take this party outside."

And with that they jumped out of the car. Before Tyreese moved around towards her, she pointed at him and commanded, "Strip Mister!"

He laughed, but did as he was told, stripping his clothes off, his large erect cock quivering with each motion.

She did the same, deftly peeling off all her clothing in under a minute. They threw their clothes into the car. The gravel felt cool under her feet.

Tyreese walked quickly around to her side of the car, holding his stiff cock.

"I want you to fuck me this way," Avery said, motioning for him to get in back of her.

She stood standing with her arms braced, one against the open door, the other against the car roof. She spread her legs out a little and stuck her big round butt out, arching her back.

Tyreese smacked her ass, and moved up behind her. Holding his dick he rubbed its prick along the inside folds of her waiting pussy, exploring her wetness, teasing her with it.

When Avery could no longer stand the anticipation commanded, "Fuck me! Just fuck me, dammit!"

"Okay," he said, and suddenly lunged forward, jamming the entire length of him inside her with one motion.

Avery gasped, and gritted her teeth as he immediately started to pound against her. Her braced arms tensed with each impact. She delighted in knowing that if she hadn't held herself in such a way, he may very well of fucked her straight through the door with his powerful thrusts.

He pounded against her, over and over, until her moans grew louder and more intense. Her flesh grew red where he smashed up against her. He smacked her ass cheek repeatedly, slapping each one in turn.

As he continued to fuck her, he licked his thumb and then rubbed it against her little ass-hole. He circled it with his thumb over and over.

Several minutes passed as he worked on her, and the forest filled with the sounds of their passionate efforts. She moaned, and occasionally yelped when he smacked her reddening flesh. He gasped, trying desperately not to cum just yet.

When he was close to being spent he slowed, easing in and out of her gently. He reached up and cupped her large tits, which spilt out over his fingers. He squeezed them, and pinched at her erect sensitive nipples.

Then, he pulled out of her, and smacked her ass loudly one more time.

"Ow!" she cried with delight.

"I want to eat your pussy," he said pointing towards the hood of the car.

She glowed. "Great idea!"

Avery giggled as she tiptoed to the front of the car. He followed in hot pursuit, eyes on the voluptuous prize. The hood was sloped and she eased herself up it by wiggling her bum. Then she leaned back on her elbows and spread her legs.

The fibreglass popped and sagged with her weight.

"I don't think this car was designed for this," Avery said, not caring in the least.

"Let's see what else it wasn't designed for," Tyreese said with mischievous smile. He squatted in front of her, placing those strong hands against her widened thighs, then he leaned forward and gave her shaved pussy a nice long welcoming lick.

Then he licked again, and again, until he developed a rhythm. Avery bent her head back and smiled gloriously up at the blue morning sky, enjoying the sensation of his tongue all over her pussy.

Eventually, he sucked on one of his fingers to get it wet, then he cautiously slipped it up inside her, and she gasped. Then he started to make a come-hither motion against the sensitive pad just behind her pubic bone. She shivered with pleasure, practically seeing stars before her eyes with the intensity.

He returned to work, concentrating more now on her clit. He sucked at it, tickling it with his tongue at the same time. All the while, she gasped with pleasure, squeezing her tits, pinching at their erect nipples. She took one in her mouth and teethed it, sucking.

He ate her out for long moments, listening to the wet sounds his gyrating finger made inside her.

When he had his fill he then stood, cock hard and ready. He leaned forward, so he was hovering over her, and bent his dick downward as far as it would go. He stuck his prick into her waiting pussy. She gasped, and grabbed onto his hips.

"You want this?" he asked.

"Yes!" she begged. "Fuck the hell outta me!"

And with that, he suddenly slammed the entire length of his long black dick deep inside her. She gasped with the hard penetration. He then lifted his ass up again, so his entire dick was nearly unsheathed from her, and slammed it down again.

The hood of the car popped and squawked with the hard pressured movements.

Over and over he did this, getting faster and faster. She moaned with each pelvic thrust. Long wonderful minutes passed as he slammed her pussy again and again. Eventually, the intensity got to be so much Avery's eyes rolled upwards, completely lost in the rapture of the moment.

Over and over; again and again he slammed down onto her.

He could not keep up the relentless pace. With both the feeling of the rubbing wet friction inside her, and seeing her face grimace with the concentrated effort of their passion, he found himself about to orgasm.

“I'm gonna cum!” he finally shouted.

Quickly, Avery pushed him back, unsheathing him form her.

Tyreese stood before her, stroking his long cock vigorously. Sitting on the edge of the hood, she leaned forward so she could place the bottom of her open mouth against the base of his prick. Her tongue tickled at it eagerly, and her eyes stared up at him with hunger.

He stroked faster, and soon came with a loud moan. His semen spat out all over her; hot squirts into her mouth which slid down her tongue and pooled at the back of her throat. Over her face in long sticky strands that splayed across her cheeks and forehead. In the corner of one eye, down her chin, and he even got some in her hair. Her large tits were spattered with his hot cum as well.

As Tyreese sagged with completion, she made a dramatic show of swallowing.

She smacked her mouth, and rolled her tongue around her lips, getting every white bit. A long thick strand still hung from her chin as she grinned widely at him.

She then grabbed his big dick, and sucked it as his erection faded, nursing the last of his load.

Looking up at his handsome face, seeing the sunshine glint off the sweat on his muscular chest, she came to a conclusion:

She needed to almost run over dark handsome men more often!

END

www.ingramcontent.com/pod-product-compliance
Ingram Content Group UK Ltd.
Pitfield, Milton Keynes, MK11 3LW, UK
UKHW021934190726
13853UKWH00004B/1442

9 798201 358754